FOR THE PEREZ-JUCKES FAMILY

This edition first published in the United Kingdom in 2014
by Pavilion Children's Books
an imprint of the Anova Books Group Ltd
10 Southcombe Street
London
W14 0RA

Associate Publisher: Ben Cameron
Designer: Claire Marshall
Editor: Kate Baker
Production Controller: Helen Gerry

ISBN: 978-1-84365-276-2

A CIP catalogue record for this book is available from the British Library.

10 9 8 7 6 5 4 3 2 1

Reproduction by Rival Colour Ltd, UK
Printed and bound in China by Ocean Printing

This book can be ordered directly from the publisher online at
www.anovabooks.com

DINOSAUR BEACH

Frann PreSton - Gannon

It's the holidays and you're off to the beach!
So much needs to be done. You must pack
all of the buckets and spades, and
prepare a lovely picnic lunch.

Then get everyone ready.
Count to make sure no one is missing.
1 ... 2 ... 3 ... 4 ... 5

It won't take long to get there.
Who will be the first to see the sea?

Make sure everyone carries
something down to the beach.

It's important to make
sure everyone gets a
swim before lunch.

Then it's finally time for your picnic.

Three extra large ice creams and
two lollies please!

OH NO!

The tide is coming in!

If anyone needs help,
remember to work together.

Best of all, you can make
new friends at the beach.

When the sun starts to set it's time to say goodbye and head back home.

We all had
ice cream!!!

We made
14 sandcastles

Shrinking Mouse 2022

THDRAWN

PAT HUTCHINS

Shrinking Mouse

RED
FOX

A Red Fox Book

Published by Random House Children's Books
20 Vauxhall Bridge Road, London SW1V 2SA

A division of The Random House Group Ltd
London Melbourne Sydney Auckland
Johannesburg and agencies throughout the world

Copyright © Pat Hutchins 1997

1 3 5 7 9 10 8 6 4 2

First published in the United Kingdom by The Bodley Head Children's Books, 1998

Red Fox edition 2001

Printed in Singapore by Tien Wah Press (PTE) Ltd

THE RANDOM HOUSE GROUP Limited Reg. No. 954009

www.randomhouse.co.uk

ISBN 0 09 940056 1

For Les
and
Mary Beckett

Fox, Rabbit, Squirrel, and Mouse were sitting at the edge of their wood, looking across the fields. "Look at that tiny wood over there," said Mouse. "It's even smaller than I am. And look, there's Owl flying towards it."

"Oh, dear!" said Fox. "He's shrinking.
I'll go and tell him to come back
before he disappears altogether."
And Fox set out after Owl.

"Oh, dear!" cried Rabbit. "Fox is shrinking, too. I'll go and tell him to come back before he disappears like Owl!"
And Rabbit set off after Fox.

"Oh, dear!" cried Squirrel.
"Rabbit is shrinking, too!
I'll go and tell him to come back
before he disappears like Fox!"
And Squirrel set off after Rabbit.

Poor Mouse was very upset.
"Squirrel is shrinking, as well!" he
thought. "I must try and stop him
before he disappears like the rest
of my friends."
And Mouse scampered after Squirrel.

"The wood is getting bigger," thought Mouse. "I must be shrinking, too!" Poor Mouse didn't want to be any smaller, but he kept on running.

"The wood is really big now," thought Mouse. "I must have nearly disappeared!" Mouse didn't want to disappear, but he kept on running.

And when he got to the wood, there were Owl and all his friends.

"Have I disappeared?" asked Mouse.

"No," they said. "You're just the right size!"

"Good," said Mouse. "Let's go home." But when he turned to look at their wood, it was very, very small.

"Oh," Mouse cried. "Our wood has shrunk, too! We can't go home!"

"Follow me," said Owl.
So they did.

And as they got closer
to their wood, it got bigger. . .

and bigger.

"Are we getting smaller?"
asked Mouse.
"No," said Owl as they reached
their wood. "We're all just the
right size."
And he flew away.

"Oh, dear!" said Fox.
"Owl is shrinking again."
"Don't worry," said Mouse.
"I'm sure he'll be the right size
 when he comes back."

And he was.